This Book is Presented to:

Chloe

Name

Design-A-Bookmark
Contest Winner

Wed, Dec 27th, 2023

Date

tpl: **toronto**
public library

Two Green Birds

TWO
GREEN
BIRDS

Geraldo Valério

Groundwood Books
House of Anansi Press
Toronto / Berkeley

Published in Canada and the USA in 2023 by
Groundwood Books / House of Anansi Press
groundwoodbooks.com

We gratefully acknowledge for their financial support of our publishing program the Canada Council for the Arts, the Ontario Arts Council and the Government of Canada.

**Canada Council
for the Arts** **Conseil des Arts
du Canada**

With the participation of the Government of Canada
Avec la participation du gouvernement du Canada | **Canadä**

**ONTARIO ARTS COUNCIL
CONSEIL DES ARTS DE L'ONTARIO**
an Ontario government agency
un organisme du gouvernement de l'Ontario

Library and Archives Canada Cataloguing in Publication
Title: Two green birds / Geraldo Valério.
Names: Valério, Geraldo, author.
Identifiers: Canadiana (print) 20220273979 | Canadiana (ebook) 20220273995 | ISBN 9781773067957 (hardcover) | ISBN 9781773067964 (EPUB)
Classification: LCC PS8643.A422 T96 2023 | DDC jC813/.6—dc23

Design by Michael Solomon
Printed and bound in China

Groundwood Books is a Global Certified Accessible™ (GCA by Benetech) publisher. An ebook version of this book that meets stringent accessibility standards is available to students and readers with print disabilities.

Groundwood Books is committed to protecting our natural environment. This book is made of material from well-managed FSC®-certified forests, recycled materials and other controlled sources.

MIX
Paper from
responsible sources
FSC® C144853
FSC
www.fsc.org

With fond appreciation of Ariel Gore.
And with special thanks to Shelley Tanaka.

1
You Will
Love It

"Francisco, eat and get ready to go to your grandma's house," my mother said. "She has something to show you. I think you will love it."

"What is it?" I asked.

"It's a surprise," my mother said.

I ate my lunch quickly.

What did Grandma have to show me? I wondered.

Maybe it was a stamp album.

Weeks ago, Grandma found some old letters. She showed me how to peel the stamps off the envelopes. We soaked them in cold water. We laid them on a clean kitchen towel to dry.

I was keeping my stamps in a little cardboard box, but Grandma said I needed a stamp album.

"Maybe you'll get one as a birthday gift," she told me.

But my birthday was months away …

I finished my lunch and brushed my teeth quickly.

"I made some cornbread for you and your grandmother to eat later," my mother said.

Grandma Antonia didn't live far away, and I could walk to her house in ten minutes. If I walked really fast, I could be there even sooner.

My mother placed the cornbread on a dish and wrapped it in a tea towel. I held the bread in my arms. I held it firmly but gently, like I would hold a little kitten. The white towel felt warm and soft. It smelled of butter and cornmeal.

Grandma Antonia was seventy years old, and she lived alone. We always had things to do. We worked in the garden or we walked downtown to buy needles and thread for her embroidery. Sometimes we went to the grocer to buy coffee, butter and crackers.

Some days Grandma stopped at church. In the afternoons the church was empty and quiet. Grandma took her rosary from her purse and kneeled. She closed her eyes and moved the tips of her lips when she prayed.

I would kneel next to Grandma, but instead of praying, I looked at the paintings. The walls of the church were covered with paintings of saints and angels, with sheep and horses, flowers and trees. In the largest painting behind the altar, high above in the sky there was a scene showing a flock of birds flying up to the clouds.

Where did they go? I wondered.

•

When I got to her house, Grandma was in the kitchen washing dishes. She took the cornbread that was still warm and held it to her nose.

"It smells delicious. Later I will make some coffee for us."

She put the cornbread on the table and took my hand. "But first I want to show you something."

I was excited, thinking about the stamp album.

But instead, Grandma took me to the backyard.

Hanging from the guava tree was a cage.

"Look at the gift I received yesterday," she said.

In the cage were two parakeets. They were very quiet, sitting on a perch. Their round eyes were black and watching. Their bodies were covered with smooth green feathers.

They were as green as fresh leaves, as green as the inside of an avocado, as green as the skin of a guava not yet ripe.

They were the greenest birds I had ever seen. Their round curved beaks looked like seashells.

Grandma looked at the cage and said, "Precious! Precious! Precious!"

"Grandma, my father told me that if you see a green bird, it is a sign that something good is going to happen. He said green birds bring you good luck."

"And now I have two green birds," Grandma said. "I'll have twice as much good luck."

A smile burst through the wrinkles on her face.

"They are a couple," Grandma said. "Parakeets are birds that cannot live alone."

"Do you think they are a male and a female?" I asked.

"I don't know," she said. "They look so alike. But it really doesn't matter. They have each other."

"Where did you get them?" I asked.

"I got them from Maria, the lady who sells me eggs. She lives in the country. One day I told her that I love parakeets because they are always so joyful. Then yesterday afternoon she brought them. I can't stop looking at them. They are so pretty!"

They were more than pretty. The green of their feathers kept changing from dark green to yellowish green, then to bluish green at the tip of their wings. They looked like they were glowing.

I had never seen anything as green as those parakeets. Maybe the leaves of a pumpkin bush would be greener. But the green of the pumpkin leaves didn't glow.

The parakeets seemed to be shy. They stared at me with their round dark eyes. The tips of their tails and wings were quivering.

Grandma said that one day they would get used to her. Then she would train them to come to her finger. She would take them out of the cage and walk around with them on her shoulder.

"Both of them?" I asked.

"Well, when you are at school, I will take both of them. But whenever you come here, I will let you have one."

"I guess I will have to train them, too. So they will get used to me as well."

"You are right," she said.

The parakeets were quiet inside the cage.

"Let's leave them alone for a while," Grandma said. "I need to finish washing the dishes."

In the kitchen, I sat on the long bench she kept next to the door. From there I could talk to Grandma and still watch the parakeets outside.

When I looked at them I felt something soft and warm moving inside me. It started in my chest and moved to my whole body. Then it rose to my face and made me smile — a kind of smile that you have with yourself when you think about something good.

The backyard was yellow with the strong afternoon sun, but it was shady under the guava leaves. The two parakeets sat on their perch, keeping their little bodies tightly close to each other. Sometimes they took turns scratching each other's head and neck. They gave each other little beaky kisses.

One day my parakeet would come to my

finger. I would let it walk on my arm to perch on my shoulder. I would rub its chest and neck. The parakeet would peck the tip of my ear.

Grandma and I would sit in the backyard and each of us would have our own parakeet.

Grandma finished washing the dishes. She dried them and put everything back in the cupboard.

"I can't wait to try this cornbread. Would you like some coffee?"

Good idea. I was getting hungry already.

"I will make a special coffee for you, not too strong," Grandma said. "And you like milk in it. Right?"

"Yes, please. And lots of sugar, too."

The water boiled and Grandma poured it over the coffee grounds. The steam rose like smoke. It twirled around the kitchen before it flew out the window.

The kitchen felt warmer with the smell of coffee.

Grandma unwrapped the cornbread and cut some slices.

"Let's have our coffee outside," she suggested.

We carried the bench to the yard. We took our coffee cups and some slices of cornbread.

I blew on my coffee until it was cool enough to drink.

The cornbread was so good. Its crust was brown and crunchy, and the inside was bright yellow and moist. It tasted of butter and cheese. My mother always added grated cheese to her cornbread.

I ate one slice, and then a second one. I slowly drank my coffee.

"This is so good," I said.

"Usually young children don't like coffee," Grandma said. "But you liked it the very first time. One day, when you were little, you reached for your mother's cup. She let you have a sip. After that you always reached for some coffee whenever we were having it. So we added more milk to your coffee and you liked it even more."

While we were eating our cornbread, I asked Grandma what parakeets liked to eat.

"Maria said to feed them corn flour," Grandma said. "She also said I could give them bread soaked in water. Maria told me her chickens love it."

"Grandma, chickens eat anything you give them. But do you think the parakeets will like it?"

"Well, I don't know. But let's try it."

"And corn flour is very dry," I said.

"Do you think so?"

"Yes. Have you tried to eat powdered milk? It gets stuck on the top of your mouth. It is hard to swallow. It makes you choke. You have to drink lots of water to swallow it. Corn flour might be just like powdered milk."

"I will give them plenty of water," she said. "And soaked bread is very moist, too."

"Is there anything else we could give them?" I asked.

"We could also try some collard greens. My mother had a canary and she fed it collard leaves."

We took our cups and dishes inside. While Grandma washed them, I got another slice of cornbread and sat outside to watch the parakeets.

I thought of the many ways I was going to play with them. We would walk around the house. They would climb to the top of my head and play with my hair. They would fly around the yard but they would always come back to me. We would climb the guava tree together looking for the ripest fruit.

Parakeets love guavas. Me, too. I couldn't wait until the guavas were in season.

When Grandma sent me home, she asked if I could come back the next day.

"Yes," I said. "I will be here tomorrow."

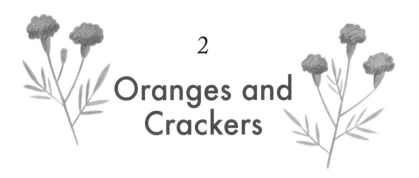

2
Oranges and Crackers

The next day I went straight to the backyard with Grandma.

The cage was hanging from the tree. Inside, the parakeets were still very quiet, squeezed together. They sat as far away from Grandma and me as they could.

"Last night I put the cage in the sewing room so the birds would be safe and warm." Grandma said. "I thought they would be more cheerful this morning. But whenever I come close to the cage, I can see their little bodies trembling."

"Do you think they are afraid of you?" I asked.

"They might be. They aren't used to us yet."

We went into the kitchen. Grandma cut an orange into pieces. The orange was juicy. Not too sweet and not too sour.

"Can I get you some crackers?" she asked. "With butter?"

"Yes, please."

For a long time I didn't like crackers. I used to think that they didn't taste like anything. I preferred cookies.

Then Grandma showed me how to spread butter on a cracker. Now I love them.

I licked my greasy fingers and asked for one more.

"The parakeets haven't eaten any of the food

I gave them. Do you think they really don't like corn flour?" Grandma asked.

"Maybe they tried it, but they choked. Then they gave up."

"I changed their water this morning. It seems that they have drunk some."

"They might have tried to eat some flour, choked and had to drink some water."

"They didn't eat the soaked bread, either."

"What about giving them some pieces of cracker?"

Grandma opened her cupboard and got a package of crackers.

I made a little pile of crushed crackers. I ate one or two crumbs before I put them in a little bowl.

I hoped the parakeets would like the crackers as much as I did.

"Grandma, let's give them some pieces of orange, too. When birds live free in nature, they eat fruit and seeds."

We walked to the guava tree. The parakeets walked fast from one end of the perch to the other. They were breathing hard, their chests moving up and down.

"Francisco, let's work quickly. I will open the door of the cage. Then you can put in the crackers and oranges," Grandma said very quietly.

First I removed the wet bread. Then I placed the new food in.

We hung the cage back in the guava tree. We watched the birds for a while. They stared at us the whole time, never going to the bottom of the cage to eat.

The parakeets just sat on their perch, watching.

"Let's go to the garden," Grandma said.

Grandma and I worked on the marigold patch.

The bushes had grown a lot, and they were all covered with orange flowers. Some of the bushes were starting to bend with so much weight. Grandma stuck some bamboo poles in the ground and tied the marigold stems to them.

"This way, when it rains, the branches won't break," she said.

I liked helping Grandma with the marigolds.

We finished our work in the garden.

"If I know you, you are probably hungry, aren't you?" Grandma said.

"Yes, I am."

While Grandma made the coffee, I watched the birds. I never saw them jump off their perch. I never saw them stretch their wings and make parakeet noises.

They were quiet, but they also preened each other, combing the feathers on their heads, necks and chests. It was so sweet.

We had our coffee in the kitchen. Left-over cornbread tasted as good as it did the day before. Grandma also gave me some crackers with butter.

I dipped my cracker in my coffee. I liked how it tasted. I did it over and over again.

The butter melting on the warm coffee made circles of grease on the surface of my drink.

3

Polenta and Greens

The next day, Grandma opened the door for me. She didn't look too happy.

"How arc the parakeets?" I asked.

"I'm not sure."

We went to the backyard. The birds in the cage were the same as the day before. They were very quiet, squeezing their little shaking bodies together.

Grandma looked at me and raised her eyebrows.

"Grandma, did they at least try some of the food?"

"Nothing, Francisco," she said. "They are just drinking water."

"That's good."

"I think we should try to feed them something else," Grandma suggested. "I have seen people feeding their birds polenta. And polenta is cornmeal and water cooked together."

"Yes," I said. "Let's do it!"

Grandma opened her cupboards.

"Francisco, I'm out of cornmeal. Run to Rosa next door and ask to borrow some. Here, take this cup with you."

"Grandma, let's ask Dona Rosa for collard greens, too. Do you remember that your mother fed collard greens to her canary?"

"Why didn't I think of that? Collard greens!

Just like my mother used to do." Grandma was smiling now.

Dona Rosa and Grandma had been neighbors for years. Dona Rosa didn't grow her plants the way Grandma did, in flower beds.

In her garden, things grew everywhere. Her whole garden was one big flower bed with a yellow house in the middle.

As soon as I came through the gate, her little yapping dog came running to check on me. Pituca barked and barked like he was the fiercest wolf. But he was so tiny. I wasn't afraid of him.

"Pituca! Stop it!" Dona Rosa shouted at her dog. "Come on in, Francisco."

I walked through the garden. Pituca ran ahead, yapping and jumping.

"Hi, Dona Rosa." I waved the teacup in my hand. "Grandma asked if you had some cornmeal. She is making polenta for her new parakeets."

"How are they doing? I saw the birds on Sunday when Maria came over with them. They are so pretty."

Pituca walked around me, sniffing my feet.

"The birds are not eating the food we gave them," I said. "Grandma is going to make them some polenta. She also asked if you could give her a couple of leaves of collard green."

"I'd be glad to. Follow me."

Dona Rosa walked around picking all kinds of collard greens. Some leaves were bright green and some purplish green. Some had jagged leaves.

I didn't know there were so many kinds.

Dona Rosa kept picking leaves, and my arms were already full.

"Dona Rosa, I think this is enough. The birds are quite small," I said.

"You can take some to your mother, too."

Dona Rosa kept gathering other kinds of leaves — lettuce, mustard greens, kale, spinach.

Soon I had so many greens in my arms that I had to stretch my neck to see in front of me.

"You look like a walking collard bush," Dona Rosa laughed. "Now come with me. I will get you some cornmeal."

We walked to the house. Pituca ran ahead of us, yapping.

Dona Rosa put the greens in a bamboo basket. Instead of giving me one cup of cornmeal, she handed me a whole bag.

"Your grandmother will have to cook polenta for the birds tomorrow and the day after, right? So she will need some extra."

Dona Rosa took me to the front gate. She held Pituca in her arms. She scratched the back of his head, and his eyes closed slowly.

Soon I would carry the parakeets in my arms and scratch their heads, and they would look as happy as Pituca in Dona Rosa's arms.

•

"How many parakeets does Rosa think we have?" Grandma said when she saw the basket in my arms.

"She gave me extra to take home to my mother. She gave me okra for my father, too. He will cook it with lots of garlic, and my mother will make caldo verde with lots of collards."

"What about the cornmeal?"

"Here. She sent you a whole bag so you can make polenta all week."

Grandma picked out some leaves of collard greens and put them in a jar with water by the window.

It looked like a bouquet of shiny leaves. Some were wet with drops of water, and when the sun shone on them, they sparkled.

The parakeets would eat them and glow even brighter.

I watched Grandma make polenta. When I had parakeets of my own, I would already know how to cook their food.

Grandma measured some water and put it to boil over a low fire. Then she added the cornmeal.

She stirred the polenta with her wooden spoon. She stopped stirring, and I watched it cook. Little by little, bubbles started to pop in the middle.

Pop-pop! Pop-pop!

The polenta started to spit up like a little volcano.

"Here," Grandma said. "Now it is your turn to stir."

I slowly stirred the polenta. As it cooked, it spat more and more. A large blob of hot polenta landed on my forearm.

"Ouch," I said.

"Let me finish it," Grandma said. "From now on it will spit a lot. It is almost done."

Grandma knew when it was ready. She took it off the stove and poured the polenta on a plate to cool. A curtain of steam rose from the yellow polenta.

"Grandma, can I try some?"

"Wait a few minutes," she said. "Let's place the dish on the windowsill. The polenta will cool faster."

We went outside. We sat on the wooden bench next to the kitchen door. We didn't want to be too close to the guava tree. We didn't want to scare the birds.

The sun had been hot and very bright. It was good to sit in the shade. I could feel the sweat on my back dry up when I leaned against the cool wall.

"Francisco, these birds have to eat soon." Grandma said. "I don't want them to get sick."

"Grandma, they will eat the polenta and the crackers. I think they will love the collard greens and the oranges, too."

Grandma took my hand in hers and gently squeezed it. "I hope so."

We sat and watched the parakeets in their cage. They were so quiet, it looked like they were sleeping.

Then Pituca started to bark behind the fence from Dona Rosa's garden.

"Pituca!" Dona Rosa called. "Come here, you naughty boy."

Grandma looked at me and smiled.

"He is a cute naughty dog. Don't you think so?"

"He is very naughty," I said. "And, Grandma, you'll see. Once the parakeets get to know us and start to eat, they will be cute and naughty, too."

"I'm very much looking forward to playing with our naughty parakeets. Let's check the polenta."

The polenta was cool. Grandma cut it into pieces and gave me one.

I put the whole piece in my mouth.

"Grandma, it is very soft. It melts in your mouth."

Grandma put some polenta on a dish. She picked one small leaf of collard green.

We went to the yard. When Grandma lowered the cage to the ground, the parakeets walked back and forth on the perch, always keeping their eyes on Grandma and me. When they bumped into the metal bars of the cage, they walked back on the perch until they reached the bars on the other side.

I spoke with my softest voice. "We are just bringing you some food."

They didn't seem to listen to me. They kept walking like two little parakeet robots.

Grandma handed me the dish with the polenta. I knew what to do.

As quietly as I could, I opened the door of the cage and quickly placed the little dish inside.

But when Grandma put the leaf of collard green inside the cage, the parakeets got very scared. They flapped their wings and flew straight into the side of the cage, like they wanted to push themselves through the bars to fly away. They lost some feathers. I felt scared for them.

"Shh, shh. It's okay," Grandma murmured quietly. But I could see that she was upset, too.

Grandma and I hung the cage back in the tree.

The parakeets stood on their perch catching their breath. Their little chests rose up and down.

Their eyes looked bigger, like dark circles of fear.

4

A Bag
of Seeds

In the morning, I helped my mother bake an orange cake for Dona Rosa. When my mother took it out of the oven, she poured orange juice over the warm cake, and she let me sprinkle sugar on top of it. She said that if someone sent you a plate or a basket with a gift, you should give them a treat to thank them.

My mother baked a little cake for Grandma, too.

"Take the basket to Dona Rosa as soon as you get to your grandmother's. Tell her that I am very grateful for all the vegetables she sent me."

At Grandma's, I ran straight to the backyard. But when I came close to the cage, the parakeets were trembling.

I walked back to the house. Grandma was in the kitchen.

"Have they eaten?" I asked Grandma.

"Not a thing," she said. "This morning I went to Rosa's to thank her for the cornmeal. I told her that I didn't know what to do to make the birds eat. She suggested that I go to the pet store. They sell birds there, and Rosa said they will certainly know what to do. I was just waiting for you to arrive."

"Good idea," I said. "Let's go now. I'll take Dona Rosa's basket to her when I get back. The sooner we find the food for the birds the better."

Before we left, Grandma made me drink some water.

"The sun is very hot today," she said. "I will bring my umbrella."

We left the house, closing the front gate behind us. I held onto Grandma's arm and our feet walked side by side on the dusty sidewalk. Grandma wore her flat black shoes, and I wore my green flip-flops.

We walked together under the shade of her umbrella with our faces hidden from the sun.

•

The pet store looked like a cage you could walk into. There were birds everywhere. The whole place was filled with piping, chirping and cackling. It smelled of dust and feathers.

In the middle of the store were some large cages with black ducks and long-necked white geese. There were chickens and roosters, too. Some were white, some orange, some brown. The black turkeys were huge, and their necks had dangly red skin that looked like warts.

The Guinea fowls were the most amazing. Their feathers were dark gray and covered with white dots. Their faces were white and had some red lumps sticking out from their cheeks. Their heads had a bump that looked like a helmet.

There were cages filled with yellow canaries. There were white and gray finches. More cages were crowded with doves and pigeons.

Then I heard the loudest clatter behind me. When I turned around, I saw a very large cage filled with parakeets.

These parakeets were a bit different from the ones Grandma and I had. They were smaller.

Some of them had green feathers. Some were yellow. The blue ones had black speckles all over their wings and tails. Some were very white.

A few of them had many colors on their bodies.

They were noisy and playful, flying from perch to perch.

One day our parakeets would be like this, too.

Grandma was already talking to the salesman at the counter.

"I have been given two wild parakeets, and they aren't eating anything." She told him about all the different kinds of food we had tried.

"I have just what you are looking for."

The salesman pulled a bag of seeds from the shelf behind the counter.

"Your birds will love this assortment of seeds," he said. "If I were you, I would throw away the crackers and polenta, but I would continue to give them the fruit and greens."

"This is wonderful news," Grandma said. "I'll take one bag."

"Is there anything else you might need today?" he asked. "What about a large cage? Look at this one right here. It has plenty of space for the birds to exercise."

"Today I will take just the seeds," she said.

"Grandma, come here. I want to show you something." I pointed to the small parakeets in the cage.

"Oh, how lovely! You see? That's why I love parakeets. They are the most joyful of birds. I can't wait for our parakeets to be as loud and happy as these."

We rushed back to the house. Grandma found a little stone bowl in her cupboard, and I filled it with seeds.

The parakeets squeezed closer together. They never took their eyes off us. But at least they didn't flap their wings against the wire bars.

I threw away the polenta and the crumbled

crackers. I changed the water, too. Grandma gave them a fresh leaf of collard green.

The parakeets were shaking. It made me sad that they were so scared of us.

We walked away from the guava tree and watched them from the kitchen.

"Look, Grandma! Can you see them stretching their necks? I think they are curious about the seeds."

"I hope so, Francisco."

Grandma stared at the cage. Her eyes looked like they were looking at something very far away.

"Grandma, the parakeets are going to eat all the seeds. You'll see. Tomorrow we will have to fill the bowl again."

She smiled. "Go and take Rosa's basket, and her cake, too."

•

When I got back from Dona Rosa's, Grandma had set the table. I ate a slice of cake and some crackers with butter. I was so hungry.

"I keep looking at the parakeets in the cage, Francisco," Grandma said. "They haven't left their spot. They haven't eaten any of the seeds."

I was worried, too.

"Grandma, maybe they're not hungry because they don't exercise," I said. "The parakeet cage at the pet store had a lot of space for the birds to fly and move around. What if we get a bigger cage? In a bigger cage they can jump from one side to the other. Maybe they can even fly a little bit. And they will get hungry from all this exercise."

"Do you think so?"

"Yes, I do."

5

A Cage

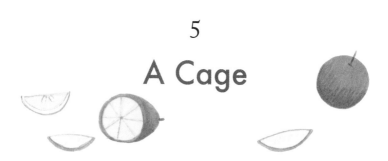

The next morning, I got up early. I couldn't wait to go to Grandma's.

My feet walked as fast as they could. By the time I arrived at Grandma's, my neck was dripping with sweat.

Grandma was in the front yard watering her garden.

"How are the parakeets this morning?" I asked.

"Oh, Francisco, nothing has changed."

I ran to the back of the house. I saw the birds sitting quietly in their cage.

I went back to Grandma.

"Francisco, I was thinking about what you said. If the birds have a larger cage, they might feel better. They might move around more, get hungry and then eat. I think this is the only thing we can do for them. I will buy a larger cage."

•

"You're back!" The pet-store man greeted us right at the door of the store. He was arranging a display of cages on the sidewalk.

"I came to look at the larger cage you showed me yesterday," Grandma said.

The salesman took us to the back of the store. I walked past the colorful parakeets. Many of them were gathered around a large bowl of seeds. They couldn't stop chattering, even when they were eating. There was so much joy inside that large cage.

That's it, I thought. Our birds just need a bigger house.

Grandma had already chosen her cage.

"I want this one," she said. "It is strong but light enough for me to carry by myself."

It was not as big as the one with the parakeets in the store, but it was larger than the one we had.

Grandma made arrangements to have the cage delivered.

"I will be there in one hour," the man said.

It didn't take long for the cage to arrive. The pet-store man brought it to the backyard under the guava tree. Grandma showed him the parakeets.

"What beauties they are," he said. "I'm sure

they'll do well in the new cage. Give them some time. They'll get used to eating their seeds, too."

Grandma and I stood in front of the large, square cage. It stood high off the ground on four strong legs. There was a door at the front.

The cage came with two feeders and a water dispenser. It had three wooden perches.

The parakeets would be able to jump up and down all day long. They would be able to flap their wings and fly from one perch to another.

The first thing we did was clean the cage. Grandma got a cloth and dusted it. I filled the feeders with seeds and filled the water dispenser.

The cage was ready for the parakeets.

"Francisco, how are we going to move the birds into the new cage?"

"I know what to do," I said. "You will pull open the door of the large cage. Then I will hold the little cage with the parakeets right in front of it. Once the cages are facing each other, I will pull open the gate of the smaller cage."

"It sounds good to me," Grandma said. "Let's do it."

We placed both cages with their open doors facing each other. I was the one holding the cage with the parakeets, so I had to make them move.

I banged my hand against the bars. The birds flew inside their little cage, crashing their bodies against the metal wires. They were so scared of me and Grandma, and of the big new cage in front of them.

I tapped my hand more softly against the cage. The parakeets moved around until they landed on the floor right in front of the open doors. I could see their beating hearts bouncing up and down underneath their green chests. My heart was also beating fast.

"Shoo, go, go … shoo, shoo … move, move," I said very gently.

And quietly they started to move. They took one, two steps. On their third step they were almost inside the larger cage.

"Shoo, shoo … go, go …"

And they walked all the way into the new cage.

They flapped their wings and jumped to the perch at the very top.

And there they stayed.

"I guess it will take them time to get used to their new house," Grandma said. "Now I will make us some lunch."

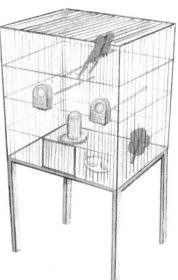

I sat outside, waiting to see the parakeets jump from perch to perch, to fly around the cage and eat the seeds from the feeders.

But again they just sat quietly on their perch. They did not bother with any of the food we gave them.

They did not care about the new cage.

They sat as before, quiet and still, but now in a bigger cage.

Grandma came to call me to eat. We sat at the table to eat rice and beans with sauteed collard greens. Grandma warmed up some of the leftover polenta. She cooked some sausages, too.

The lunch was delicious. I had two servings.

Grandma peeled oranges for dessert. They were so juicy. The parakeets would have liked them. My fingers were moist and sticky with the juice of the oranges.

Grandma was quiet. I knew she was thinking about the parakeets.

Grandma washed the dishes and I dried them. It didn't take too long. She swept and mopped the floor. The whole kitchen still smelled of oranges.

Grandma looked out at the guava tree. We both knew that the birds were not eating. They were not playing in the larger cage. It was all very quiet in Grandma's backyard.

By then the sun wasn't shining anymore. The sky had become cloudy.

"Look." Grandma pointed at the sky. "I think you should go home before the rain starts."

Before I left, I helped Grandma bring the large cage inside.

The birds had not touched any of the food.

"The man from the pet store said that as soon as the parakeets got used to the cage, they would start eating. When do you think they will get used to it?" I asked Grandma.

"I don't know."

I looked at the parakeets and I wondered if they were getting thinner. I couldn't tell.

I walked back home. I walked fast. The clouds in the sky were moving faster.

The wind was blowing strong, bringing with it the smell of rain.

6
Clouds
Rolling Away

The next morning, the sky was bright blue.

When I arrived at Grandma's, she was working in the garden.

"Today would be a good day to plant these hydrangeas. It is cooler after the rain last night. The soil is nice and moist."

"How are the parakeets today?" I asked. "Did they eat their seeds?"

"Francisco, nothing has changed," Grandma sighed.

"Are they playing in the new cage?"

"Not at all," she said. "They just sit quietly in the same spot. Whenever I come close, they start to shake with fear. I don't know what else to do. Do you?"

"Grandma, I'll think of something," I said. "I'm going to take a look at them. I'll be back."

•

The new cage sat on the ground under the guava tree. There was a lot of space inside that cage. But both parakeets perched quietly, one squeezed tightly against the other. The food dispenser was full of uneaten seeds.

Nothing had changed.

"What should we do with you two?" I asked them.

But they said nothing. Their black eyes did not shine.

I started to think that they were not as green as when I first saw them. Were they thinner, too? There were a few feathers on the floor of the cage.

I started to go back to tell Grandma about the feathers.

Just as I was leaving the back garden, I heard noises behind me.

Krah, krah, krah …

The parakeets! The parakeets were screaming!

I turned around and saw both parakeets jumping from perch to perch.

They flapped their wings and screamed, *Krah, krah, krah …*

I quietly walked over to the cage and the parakeets didn't try to move away from me. They didn't look afraid anymore.

Yes! Yes! I thought. They were getting used to the cage and to me.

I was so happy. It was a great idea to get them a larger cage.

Krah, krah, krah … The parakeets screamed.

Krah, krah, krah … Their screams grew louder and louder.

Their screams were too loud.

Suddenly the whole backyard was very noisy with *krahs*.

I looked up. The whole guava tree was full of parakeets. There were dozens of parakeets.

No, more than dozens. They were jumping from branch to branch, walking all over the tree. They flapped their wings and gave each other parakeet kisses.

Krah, krah, krah … The caged parakeets screamed back. They jumped from perch to perch and flapped their wings, looking up at the parakeets in the tree.

I went to find Grandma.

"Grandma, come to the yard quickly!"

"What's going on back there?" she asked.

"You won't believe it," I said. "Come and see for yourself."

"Oh, my!" That was all Grandma said when she saw the guava tree bursting with parakeets.

"I have never seen so many parakeets together," Grandma said.

It was a loud, screeching parakeet tree.

The parakeets in the cage jumped from perch to perch, flapping their wings and screaming. I had never seen them so alive.

And then, suddenly, all the parakeets in the tree took off and flew away.

The caged parakeets called their friends back, but they did not return.

"Grandma, who were the other parakeets?"

"I don't know."

"They might know each other."

"Maybe."

"Those parakeets might have come looking for their friends."

We walked to the cage. The parakeets moved themselves to the perch in the very back, pressing their bodies against the wires of the cage. Their eyes looked so big. Their beaks were open a little bit, like when you are having a bad dream and you want to scream for help but your voice won't come out.

Our little parakeets were quivering from their tails to their wings.

"Francisco," Grandma said. "What is going to happen to these two birds?"

When the parakeets had first arrived, whenever Grandma looked at them or talked about them, her face smiled.

But now when she looked at them, the folds of her eyes melted into the wrinkles on her face. Her lips didn't smile anymore. She looked sad.

"Francisco, what should we do?"

I didn't know what to say.

We left the parakeets alone. We went back to the garden to plant the hydrangeas. I took off my sandals. It felt good to feel the earth on the bottom of my feet. I loved gardening barefoot.

Grandma showed me how I should dig the ground, softening the earth. She showed me how to plant the seedlings.

I watered the little hydrangeas.

Later we moved to the begonias. Their heart-shaped leaves were shiny like silver. Grandma talked to her begonias while she checked them for bugs. Grandma talked to plants like they were children.

We were talking about weeds and flowers,

when I started to hear noises coming from the backyard. I heard one, two, and suddenly lots of *krahs*.

In the backyard, all the parakeets were back. It looked like the tree had more parakeets than leaves. The parakeets walked up and down, over all the branches.

Krah, krah, krah …

Krah, krah, krah …

It was like a party of parakeets. They played with each other. They scratched their necks and gave each other kisses. They flapped their wings and flew among the leaves. They took over the whole tree.

The caged birds were also screaming and jumping from perch to perch. Some parakeets jumped from the tree to the top of the cage, flapping their wings and screaming.

Krah, krah, krah …

Krah, krah, krah …

One of the parakeets in the cage clawed itself onto the bar and started to climb upside down. It stretched its neck and tried to bite the wire.

Krah, krah, krah …

Krah, krah, krah …

The parakeets were talking, and we were listening.

"Francisco." Grandma's voice was very quiet. "What should we do?"

I did know what to do.

When I walked toward them, the free parakeets on top of the cage flew back into the tree. The birds inside the cage went back to their perch, walking from one side to the other, flapping their wings, too. The parakeets in the tree kept screaming.

I unlatched the door of the cage and opened it wide. I walked back and stood next to Grandma.

Krah, krah, krah … The guava tree screamed.

Inside the cage the two birds jumped from one perch to another. They flapped their wings and jumped to the floor of the cage and walked around. They came to the open door and looked outside.

They jumped from the door of the cage to the tree above. They mixed with the other parakeets.

Soon Grandma and I could not pick out which ones used to be our parakeets.

They stayed in the tree for a little while, screaming loudly and jumping from one branch to another.

And then all the parakeets took off. They flew into the sky as a large cloud of screaming birds.

Krah, krah, krah …

They all flew away.

Grandma and I walked to the middle of the yard and we looked up at the open sky.

The green birds were gone.

"They flew fast," Grandma said.

All we could see were clouds rolling away through the blue sky.

Grandma looked at me. We were both smiling.

Grandma and I emptied the seeds from the food dispenser. We threw away the pieces of orange, the collard greens and the water. We cleaned the cage and put it in the sewing room.

We went back to the garden.

There is always a lot of work to do in a garden.

GERALDO VALÉRIO was born in Brazil. *Two Green Birds* is based on his own childhood — a time he spent playing outside in the bright hot sun while loud flocks of green parakeets flew in the sky. (Also, his middle name is Francisco, and he loved to drink coffee when he was a child!)

Geraldo studied drawing in Brazil and later at New York University. He has written and illustrated many picture books, including *Night Runners*, *My Book of Butterflies*, *At the Pond*, *Friends* and *Blue Rider*. His work has been published in Canada, the US, Brazil, Portugal, France, the UK and China.

Geraldo now lives in Toronto, Ontario.

Groundwood Books is grateful for the opportunity to share stories and make books on the Traditional Territory of many Nations, including the Anishinabeg, the Wendat and the Haudenosaunee. It is also the Treaty Lands of the Mississaugas of the Credit. In partnership with Indigenous writers, illustrators, editors and translators, we commit to publishing stories that reflect the experiences of Indigenous Peoples. For more about our work and values, visit us at groundwoodbooks.com.